STANS GALACTIC BUG

Stan groaned. There must be a bug in the game, he told himself quietly, a programming error which could cause peculiar things to happen. Then the computer sound system began beeping. It usually did that when Stan made some sort of mistake. But now it was beeping madly, almost like someone talking furiously in a high-pitched voice. It sounded so comical that Stanley turned up the sound knob to hear it better.

"I demand to be set free!" said the voice, as clear as anything. "Let me out of this ridiculous prison!"

John Emlyn Edwards

STANS GALACTIC BUG

Illustrated by Caroline Jayne Church

Hippo Books
Scholastic Publications Limited
London

Scholastic Publications Ltd.,
10 Earlham Street, London WC2H 9RX, UK

Scholastic Inc.,
730 Broadway, New York, NY 10003, USA

Scholastic Tab Publications Ltd.,
123 Newkirk Road, Richmond Hill,
Ontario L4C 3G5, Canada

Ashton Scholastic Pty. Ltd.,
P O Box 579, Gosford, New South Wales,
Australia

Ashton Scholastic Ltd.,
165 Marua Road, Panmure, Auckland 6,
New Zealand

Text copyright © John Emlyn Edwards, 1989
Illustrations copyright © Caroline Jayne Church, 1989

First published 1989

ISBN 0 590 76195 1

All rights reserved

Made and printed by Cox and Wyman Ltd.,
Reading, Berks.

Typeset in Baskerville by COLLAGE (Design in Print)
Longfield Hill, Kent.

10 9 8 7 6 5 4 3 2 1

CHAPTER 1

"Stan, the meal's on the table!" shouted Mrs Wheeler from the kitchen.

Stan was not listening. He was hunched in front of the computer in his bedroom. He had just started a new adventure game, and already he was in deep trouble. The game was called The Gem of Power. It began with a message on the computer screen that read . . .

"You are imprisoned in a tower surrounded by thick forests and high mountains on the giant planet Parl which is ruled by an evil dictator called Vlast. To escape, you must find your way to the Gem of Power, which is hidden somewhere on the planet in a secret cave guarded by horrible monsters.

"Your tower is locked up in a time-and-space maze. At every step of your escape you will have to solve problems by choosing ways to go and things to do. One mistake could lead to disaster.

"Worse still, Vlast is plotting a gruesome death for you. So you dare not waste a moment in finding the Gem of Power and working out how it can help you escape. Begin now. Good luck. You'll need it."

Stan frowned and tapped the keyboard. The screen flashed up a colourful graphic display. The forests looked tropical and the mountains had snow on them. The tower was buried in a funny-looking maze. Behind an iron grille at the bottom of the tower was a star symbol ★, which told Stan exactly where he was. In deep trouble.

"Get down here, Stan! Move yourself!" This time it was Dad's voice. He sounded unusually grumpy. Stan switched off the computer, ran downstairs and joined Mum and Dad at the kitchen table for the evening meal.

"I'll have to say something to that bloke next door," muttered Dad. "He's wrecking my television programmes with those blasted gadgets of his."

6

"Doesn't bother me," said Mum. "I just watched *EastEnders*, and there was nothing wrong with the set."

"You wouldn't notice if the picture was wobbling all over the place," snorted Dad.

"Don't make a fuss, dear. Mr Day talks to people all over the world on his radio. They're a very nice family."

Stan kept out of the argument. It had been going on for weeks, ever since the Wheeler family had moved out of their old street into a semi-detached house in a newly developed area of the town. The move was Mrs Wheeler's idea. She wanted the family to get on in the world, which was also the reason why she bought Stan the second-hand computer she saw advertised in the local newspaper. Mr Wheeler, usually good-natured, was getting grumpier by the day. He was not sure they could afford the mortgage. His job at the steelworks was looking shaky. Some of his mates had already been made redundant. It could be his turn next. On top of that, he was now a long way from his beloved allotment, and the new house had a garden too small to stand a wheelbarrow on.

"I'm going out for a bit," said Stan, finishing his meal and getting up from the table.

It was quiet outside in Applecombe Avenue, not a bit like the busy street they used to live in. There were five pairs of houses in the avenue. The builders were still working on two of them. In the families that had moved in there was nobody of Stan's age. This did not worry Stan all that much. He was a bit of a loner anyway. He walked down the avenue, crossed the road and went into the grass-park area that the council had made the developers leave in the middle of the estate.

"Yeee-eh!" A triumphant yell came from a group of youngsters larking about. They were throwing stones at a row of empty glass bottles they had set up along a plank standing on two bricks. The bottles came from a builder's skip where householders had dumped them. The bricks and plank came from one of the unfinished houses.

Stan gulped and turned hastily away as he recognized them. They were a gang of toughies

8

from school who called themselves the Raiders after an American football team they watched on television, the Los Angeles Raiders. Although Stan had moved house, he still went to the same school in the centre of the town. And the worst part of school was the Raiders. They spent most of their time and all their money playing the slot machines in the amusement arcade. They bullied timid schoolmates out of their pocket-money to finance their arcade operations. When they were broke, they wandered about the new estates making a nuisance of themselves.

Stan wanted nothing to do with them. He hurried back towards the road. But he was too late. The Raiders gave a shout as they saw him, then pelted over the grass and surrounded him.

"Well, if it isn't our Stan," grunted Billy Regan, stocky leader of the Raiders.

"Stan, Stan, the new house man!" bellowed Flatnose Biggs, jigging about like a one-man pop group and pretending to play a guitar.

"He's got to be flush to live up here," said Blinker Price, squinting short-sightedly through grimy glasses.

Stan was scared stiff, but he did his best not to show it. He stuck his hands in his trouser pockets and bunched his fists like holstered guns. Small and bony, with a mop of sandy hair, he tried to make his face look tough, and he narrowed his eyes like the cowboys did in films. It did not work.

"Give us your money, or we'll thump you," snarled Billy Regan.

Stan had no money to give them, but it was no good telling them that. The Raiders would not believe him. They would make him empty his pockets and then thump him anyway. He swallowed hard and waited for the first Raiders' hand to grab him.

"What do you think you're doing?" said a voice from behind them. The Raiders whirled round. So did Stan. It was Kathy Day, the slim, attractive, nineteen-year-old daughter of the family next door. "Just you leave him alone," added Kathy, standing beside Stan and flinging back her long black hair.

"What are you going to do about it?" jeered Billy Regan.

"Yeh. Right," scoffed the other two Raiders.

Kathy gave a tug on the dog lead she was holding, and out lumbered her dog Plato. He was huge and hairy, with a savage look on his face. He glared at the Raiders and growled like thunder. Kathy bent down as if to release Plato from his lead. The Raiders turned pale and fled across the park and down the streets leading to the town.

"That's the last we'll see of them for a while," said Kathy, smiling as she saw Stan, his face even paler than usual, staring at the dog. "Plato is a softie," she told him reassuringly. "Anyway, he's on your side. Go on, give him a pat."

Still doubtful, Stan reached out a shaking hand. It felt like patting an elephant.

"I walk Plato in the park every evening," Kathy went on. "You must have seen us."

"That's right," said Stan, having forgotten it for the moment.

"He's called Plato after an ancient Greek philosopher," explained Kathy, "because he's a deep thinker too. But mostly about where his next meal is coming from."

It dawned on Stan that Kathy was chatting

away like this because she did not want to embarrass him by mentioning the fact that she had just rescued him from the Raiders. He had waved good-morning to her a few times, but this was the first conversation they had ever had. He had heard Mum say that Kathy worked in the town's biggest travel agency. To that bit of information he could now add his new discovery. Kathy was a really nice person, and very easy to get along with.

"Goodnight," said Kathy, after they had given Plato a good run in the park and walked back into Applecombe Avenue.

"Goodnight — and thanks," Stan called back, as he ran into the house.

Mum and Dad were busy. There were newspapers and catalogues and glossy brochures scattered about everywhere. They were picking out all the things they needed to buy for the new house.

"New curtains for every room, and a fitted carpet for this one," announced Mum, adding to her list. "The old carpets will do for the bedrooms. But we'll need new pots and pans."

"Give it a rest," groaned Dad. "We're not

made of money, you know."

"Bedtime, Stan," said Mum, looking up and noticing him at last. "Put the kettle on, will you?"

Stan went into the kitchen, stuck the kettle under the cold water tap and then plugged it in. It was an old kettle and it made crackling noises when he switched it on.

"You'd better put a new electric kettle on your list," advised Stan when he went back into the room.

"Whose side are you on?" complained Dad, switching the television set on to show that he was planning no more shopping that night. "Look at that," he growled disgustedly as the television screen showed a wobbly picture. "It's that bloke next door bashing away on his amateur radio. I'm not putting up with it much longer, and that's a fact."

"Take no notice," said Mum soothingly. "He's what they call a radio ham."

"I'll make ham out of him one day," threatened Dad, heading for the kitchen. "Get off to bed, Stan. I'll give you a shout when your cocoa's ready."

Stan went upstairs and switched on the computer. The Gem of Power adventure game had gripped his imagination. He tapped the keyboard and flashed up the picture of the planet Parl. There was the tower and the ★ symbol which showed where he was imprisoned. He had to escape quickly. But how was he going to thread his way through the time-and-space maze? Stan was busy selecting the right key to tap when he heard a sharp noise from the kitchen below and the lights went out.

"What's happened?" cried Mum.

"That blasted kettle has short-circuited and blown one of the main fuses!" shouted Dad, with only a vague idea of what he was talking about. "Hang on. I'll get a torch and open the fuse-box."

A few minutes later, when the lights had come back on, and the kettle slung out and water boiled in a saucepan to make the dark cocoa Stanley liked, he was back at the computer. The screen had gone crazy when the lights went out, and he had hastily switched off the machine. Now he switched it on again, hoping that no damage had been done.

The screen showed the same scene as before. Stan breathed a sigh of relief. Then he noticed something peculiar. The ★ symbol was now much bigger, throbbing and pulsating with an amazing luminosity, shining bright as a distant planet in the sky. Stan tapped several keys, instructing the ★ to leave the tower. It promptly doubled its size, flickered angrily at him and refused to move.

Stan groaned. There must be a bug in the game, he told himself glumly, a programming error which could cause peculiar things to happen. Then the computer sound system began beeping. It usually did that when Stan made some sort of mistake. But now it was beeping madly, almost like someone talking furiously in a high-pitched voice. It sounded so comical that Stanley turned up the sound knob to hear it better.

"I demand to be set free!" said the voice, as clear as anything. "Let me out of this ridiculous prison!"

Stan nearly fell off his chair. He stared round-eyed at the computer. The back of his neck went cold. He could feel his hair standing up. This was scarey.

"My name is Targ," the voice went on crossly. "I am a space traveller from the planet Karothan on the far side of the galaxy. My mission is a peaceful one. But unless you free me at once, you could well suffer terrible punishment."

Stan panicked. This game was going horribly wrong. He reached for the computer switch to turn the machine off.

"I wouldn't do that if I were you," warned Targ. "That switch could be the last thing you ever touched. Use your computer keyboard to talk back to me. Do it now!"

Stan froze. This was no game. Targ was deadly serious. He put shaking fingers on the keyboard and began tapping, slowly and carefully.

CHAPTER 2

"Hullo."

Stan looked at the message he had just typed on the computer screen. It was not exactly brilliant. But what on earth do you say to a space traveller you have just met?

"I suppose that is the best greeting I can expect from a primitive Earth dweller," snapped Targ, in his high-pitched computer-soundtrack voice.

Stan tried again. "Welcome to Earth," he typed. "How did you get into mu computer game?"

"Before I tell you that," replied Targ, "how much do you know about astro-physics and cosmology?"

"Nothing," typed Stan hastily.

"Then I'll try to make it simple," sighed Targ. "I'm a Pathfinder. I left the planet Karothan in a P2X cruise and combat craft. I was sent by the Commissioners of the Galactic Community to locate and report planets with a reasonable degree of civilization to which technical experts can go to help them develop their economy and become useful members of the Community. While crossing the galaxy, I was flung into hyper-space by a magnetic storm which also wrecked my space craft. I was forced to eject and adopt pure energy status. In this form I was transported to the Earth's atmosphere on the electro-magnetic particle waves which pervade the galaxy."

Targ paused. Stan grabbed the opportunity to sort out what he had learned so far. Amazing stuff, but it still didn't explain . . .

"As a Pathfinder, I should be used to new experiences," went on Targ suddenly. "But I confess to being startled when I found myself dragged down into a vortex made up of short-wave radio transmissions, a power shift caused by a short-circuited electric kettle and sympathetic wave-emissions from your mind."

"How did you work all that out?" typed Stan, forgetting his fears for the moment and really curious.

"I am a trained Pathfinder," squeaked Targ indignantly. "I analysed my situation in microseconds. Just as I analysed the text of your computer game, which I found to be an illogical jumble of letters forming the alphabet of a primitive language which I have adopted as the means of my communication with you."

Stan bristled. Targ seemed to be using the word primitive an awful lot when he talked about Earth dwellers.

"If you're so clever," Stan printed on the screen, "then why can't you escape all by yourself?"

He dived for the control knob and turned down the volume as Targ responded furiously. "Do not taunt me! I have the power to unleash destructive forces you have not yet dreamed of!"

"I was just asking," explained Stan, fingers flying over the keys. "What I meant was, it's only a game."

"Try using that feeble brain of yours!" scolded Targ. "I am locked into the logic of your computer game. Unfortunately it is a fantastic logic, quite unlike the pure logic I am

21

accustomed to handling. By its terms, I seem to have taken your place as prisoner in this tower on the planet Parl. I must escape before the evil dictator Vlast destroys me. You got me into this predicament. So you must get me out of it!"

Stan did some quick thinking. It was hardly fair of Targ to say that it was all his fault. All the same, Targ must be desperate. The Gem of Power might be a game to Stan, but it was a matter of life or death to Targ. Then he had a bright idea.

"What if I used the quit option and abandoned the game?" he enquired. "Wouldn't that free you?"

"Of course not!" replied Targ. "I would merely remain freeze-fixed until the next time someone switched on the game. Do not even consider it. I warn you for the last time. Help me, or you will suffer the most horrible consequences!"

Stan gazed at the ★ symbol on the computer screen which was all he could see of Targ. Even in its now enlarged form it was still pathetically small. He tried to imagine how Targ must feel, stranded on the wrong side of the galaxy and under threat of death. It was time Targ found out that primitive Earth dwellers were not quite so primitive after all. Stan reached for the keyboard.

"You don't have to threaten me," he told Targ. "I want to help you. But escaping is a problem for me too. We must help each other."

"A civilized response," replied Targ approvingly. "I'm sorry I was so angry. I thought I was dealing with a low-order form of life. I now see that I was wrong. But I would be grateful if we could begin our escape attempt immediately."

Stan tapped the keyboard and brought up on the screen the game options for escaping from the tower. They were:

(a) break down the door

(b) push out the grille

(c) tunnel under the walls.

Stan stared at the tower. The walls looked massively thick. It was take forever to tunnel under them. The door was out of sight at the back of the tower, but he guessed that it would be iron-barred and nearly as thick as the walls.

23

That left the iron grille. Stan looked carefully at it. The crossed bars did not seem to be securely fixed into the tower walls, and one or two of them did not even reach the walls. That had to be the way out of the tower. Unless it was a bluff. Which could be fatal. But they had to do something. Stan made up his mind.

"I am going to select option (b). What do you think?" he typed on the screen.

"I'm afraid I can't offer you an opinion," said Targ. "I've never broken or pushed or tunnelled in my life. Just think hard and do the best you can."

Stan felt a glow of pride. Targ was trusting him to lead the escape. Just the same, he took a deep breath before selecting option (b) with the tap of a key.

The tower shook as if there was an earthquake. For one horrible moment Stan thought it was going to crash down in ruins and bury Targ beneath tons of rubble. Then the iron grille fell out of the tower wall as though pushed by a giant hand. The ★ symbol drifted through the opening and settled on the ground outside. Targ was free from the tower.

"Well done," said Targ. "We have made a good beginning. But we still have to get through the time-and-space maze."

"I don't even understand what it is," typed Stan helplessly.

"It appears to be a simple but deadly device," reported Targ promptly, having taken only a microsecond to work it out. "You are offered many paths to take. If you choose the wrong one, you will be instantly transported to another time, maybe hundreds of years into the past or future, and another place, maybe another planet holding even more dangers than this one. The right path, of course, leads safely out of the maze."

"Wait a minute," typed Stan. He screened the game options for tackling the maze. They were simple, and not helpful:

(a) Go left
(b) Go right
(c) Go forward
(d) Go back
(e) Think about it. And get what you ask for.

Stan was baffled. The paths of the maze all looked the same. But if he sent Targ down the wrong one, he could be sent hurtling through time and space, perhaps to land on some grisly planet populated by prehistoric monsters. And if he survived, he would still be stranded forever, unable to return to Karothan.

"Well, it's obvious what we must do," decided Targ.

Stan almost fell on the floor with relief.

"Option (e) is the logical choice," went on Targ. "We must think before we move."

Stan thumped the computer desk. For one moment he thought Targ had found the solution. What was the point of having a super-brain if you couldn't work out the answer?

"I don't want to hear any more computer noises tonight, Stan," yelled Dad from the bottom of the stairs. "I want to hear toothbrushing noises from the bathroom."

Stan jumped. He had turned up the computer soundtrack to hear Targ better. But Targ had made so much noise that Mum and Dad had heard him downstairs. Stan's fingers flew over the keyboard.

"I must go. Can I switch off?" he typed.

"Certainly," answered Targ, sounding

puzzled, but logically accepting that if Stan must, then he must. "Everything will remain freeze-fixed until you return. But don't make it too long. I don't trust the evil Vlast. He could strike at any moment."

"Back soon," typed Stan in a panic, as Dad started climbing the stairs.

"Bed, Stan. This minute. Or else," growled Dad.

"I'm going. I'm going," Stan told him, switching off the computer and dashing to the bathroom.

At school the next day, the morning assembly went off much as usual. Miss Perkins, the music teacher, banged away at the piano while some pupils sang the hymns, making up funny words as they went along, and the usual crowd at the back played toe-stamping. Then the Head got up to say something. The teachers, sitting on a row of chairs behind him, glared down at the rabble, trying to make them shut up. The Head was new and very keen. They wanted to impress him. The rest of the school was not bothered.

"I have something exciting to tell you," announced the Head.

"They're shutting down the school. Hooray!" shouted a voice from the back.

"Our local travel agent has offered to run a competition," the Head went on, trying to ignore the interruption. "I want you all to enter for it. All you have to do is describe in less than a hundred words your idea of the perfect holiday."

"Don't know a hundred words," confessed a gruff voice from the middle of the hall.

"We only write on walls," screeched another.

"The winner will get us four free places on the next school trip abroad," the Head ploughed on. "I will allow the winner to give those places to anyone that he, or she, pleases."

Stan was not interested, apart from wondering if this was one of Kathy Day's ideas. He had quite enough on his plate trying to help Targ escape. Mr Bartlett, his English teacher, changed his mind for him.

"Each one of you will enter this competition, and no arguments," announced Mr Bartlett.

He was tall and lean, with a face like an angry vulture. He taught English to Stan's form, and he hated every minute of it. So did Stan's form. But that did not concern Mr Bartlett. He had put in for promotion. It would do him nothing but good if one of his pupils won the competition. "I want your entries in one week from now. And I warn you — if they are half-way intelligent, then I shall know that your parents have helped you. So don't try it on."

"Please, sir, I can't," protested Stan. "I've got too much to do at home."

"Mowing lawns and doing the washing-up, I suppose," sneered Mr Bartlett. "Pull the other leg, Stanley Wheeler, it's got bells on! Now shut up and get on with your work."

Breaktime saw Stan in even deeper trouble. The Raiders cornered him by the gymnasium.

"Get lost," said Stan, trying to sound as if he meant it. "I've got no money, and I wouldn't give it to you if I had."

"Touchy, isn't he?" grunted Billy Regan.

"Unfriendly, I call it," grinned Blinker Price.

"Shall I thump him?" snorted Flatnose

29

Biggs, bunching his fists and scowling.

"Nah," said Billy Regan. "I want him all in one piece, so's he can do this little job for us."

"What job's that?" asked Stan, curious and worried.

"That computer of yours," said Billy Regan.

"Now just a minute . . ." began Stan, alarmed at any threat to his computer, particularly now.

"Clever things, computers, I shouldn't wonder," carried on Regan, ignoring him. "I bet that computer could help you write the winning entry for the travel competition. In fact, I'm willing to bet your life on it, Stan."

"You've got his attention now," giggled Blinker.

"He's staring at you pop-eyed," sniggered Flatnose.

"No messing about. You're going to win that competition, Stan," ordered Regan, "You're going to use that computer of yours to write a really posh entry. And when you've won those free tickets, you're going to share them with us. One ticket for you and three tickets for the Raiders. Got it?"

"But you don't understand," Stan started to explain.

"No. It's you that doesn't understand," said Regan, suddenly becoming serious and prodding a hard finger into Stan's chest. "Because if you *don't* win, and we *don't* get those free tickets, then the Raiders are going to make your life really miserable."

"Better get busy, Stan," jeered Blinker nastily as he hurried after Regan, who was already stalking away.

"Ta, ta, Stan," scoffed Flatnose, shoving him against the gym wall.

Stan walked home after school. He could have taken the school bus, but he wanted to be by himself. He had a lot to think about.

"Hullo. It's Stanley Wheeler, isn't it? I thought I recognized you," said a voice as a car drew up to the edge of the pavement alongside him.

Stan whipped round. A man was leaning out of the car window and smiling at him. Mum and Dad had told him exactly what to do in a

situation like this: say nothing, keep walking, and if the man tries to get out of the car and grab you, run like mad and shout your head off.

"My name's David. I sold you your house, remember?" called out the man.

Stan puffed out his cheeks in relief. Of course he remembered this young man, David. He worked for a local estate agent. He had shown them round the house in Applecombe Avenue and arranged the purchase of it. David was serious and a bit boring, but nice and friendly.

"Hop in," said David. "I'm going your way." And as they drove off with Stan sitting in the passenger seat beside him, David murmured, "Three bedroom, semi-detached, lounge diner, fitted kitchen, prime site on new development."

"Eh?" muttered Stan, mystified.

"The house I sold your parents. Just like the one next door, where the Day family lives," went on David. "Met Kathy Day, have you?"

"Yes," answered Stan. "She's nice."

"She's more than nice, she's fantastic," said David dreamily.

Stan said nothing. But he was thinking a lot. What a silly way to carry on. How completely boring. That sort of thing. Not until the car turned into Applecombe Avenue did he pay any more attention to what David was saying. And then he had to, because David slammed the car to a halt and gasped.

Kathy Day was leaving her house. It was her afternoon off from the travel agency. But what made David react was the snappy sports car she was climbing into and the handsome young man who was driving it.

"Thanks for the lift," said Stan, climbing out. When David made no reply, he slung his school bag over his shoulder and walked towards his own house. Kathy called him over to the sports car.

"I want you to meet Mark," smiled Kathy. "Mark is in the security business. Very hush-hush."

"Hi, Stan," greeted Mark, looking James Bondish in a grey suit and tweed cap. He was blue-eyed and good-looking, a bit like somebody on TV. "Kathy has told me all about you. We'll talk soon. Must dash now.

Cheers."

He revved up the car and drove off, with Kathy waving as they went. David sat slumped behind the wheel, looking very fed up as he watched them go. Stan shrugged. It was nothing to do with him, he thought. Wrongly as it turned out. But just now he had more urgent things on his mind. He walked into the kitchen, and found Mum in a panic.

"I've got to go out, Stan," said Mum, stuffing things into her handbag and looking smart in her best outfit. "Dad'll be home soon. There's some cake in the cupboard. Bye."

Must be important, thought Stan, as she hurried out. He cut himself a wedge of cake and ran upstairs. With a bit of luck he would be left alone to concentrate on Targ. He switched on the computer and fed in the Gem of Power adventure game. To his relief, the ★ symbol showing Targ's whereabouts was standing on the ground outside the tower, bright and luminous, just where he had left it.

"How are you getting on?" typed Stan hopefully.

"Considering the rough logic I am forced to

deal with," replied Targ instantly in his high-pitched squawk, "quite well, I think. We decided to think about the time-and-space maze problem, did we not? Well, it seems to me that the maze is like a locked door. Therefore it must have a key. Now this key could be a verbal or numeric password, or a mathematical equation, or something so obvious that only an Earth dweller's primitive thinking could spot it. Have you any suggestions?"

Targe had a nerve talking about Earth intelligence like that, thought Stan. After all, he was leading the escape, wasn't he? All the same, he decided to look for an obvious solution to the problem, which was a key. He stared at the screen. No key in sight . . . except . . . what about the tower?. He had been given the option of breaking down the door. So there must be a locked door somewhere round the back of the tower. And there could be a key in the lock on the outside of the door. Stan felt a tingle of excitement.

He selected option (e) and typed out the command: "Give me the key to the tower door."

At once, a large iron key flashed up on to the screen beside Targ.

"What is that thing?" cried out a startled Targ.

"It's only the key to the maze," typed Stan, trying to make it seem easy. "Not bad for Earth intelligence, don't you think? Now it's your turn. What do we do with it?"

Determined not to be outdone, Targ took even fewer microseconds than usual to find the answer. "The key fits one of the crooked paths of the maze," he pointed out. "So the key can open the maze-lock. Try it."

Stan typed in the command: "Open the maze-lock with the key." Immediately he was presented with the screen options:

(a) Open time-and-space maze in present location

(b) Re-locate maze anywhere you choose.

Stan instantly made up his mind. He wanted the maze as far away as possible. He selected (b) and typed the command: "Relocate the maze around a distant swamp on the planet Parl." One key-stroke later, the maze had vanished.

"Well done!" Targ congratulated him. "Now we are free to search for the secret cave containing the Gem of Power."

Stan did not hear. He was staring at the screen in horror. Out of the forest was emerging something so ghastly that he could hardly believe what he was looking at. He had got Targ out of the tower and past the time-and-space maze only to place him in deadly peril. With shaking fingers, Stan rattled the keyboard and typed out a frantic message.

"Look out behind you!"

CHAPTER 3

From out of the thick forest that surrounded the tower were coming strange and horrible creatures. They looked like giant insects, with scaly bodies and long scorpion-tails that curved upwards and ended in wicked-looking claws. They were rushing towards Targ as if to gobble him up.

"You've got to help me! Do something!" yelled Targ.

Stan froze. Only a moment before he had been clever and heroic. Now he felt stupid and paralysed. The sight of the dreadful forest creatures had scared the wits out of him.

"H-e-l-p!" Targ's last wailing cry was only one notch below supersonic.

Stan forced himself to think. Scared he may have been, but Targ, about to be gobbled up, was a lot worse off. He jabbed at the computer keyboard with numb fingers and called up the

40

game options on to the screen. They told him:

(a) get back inside the tower

(b) go to the high mountains.

Stan made up his mind in a flash. Thumping a key, he selected option (b). The tower and the forests and the ghastly creatures vanished. The screen now showed a rocky trail snaking up the side of a snow-crested mountain. The ★ symbol showing Targ's whereabouts was perched halfway up the trail, on the edge of a precipice. Far below, looking like a tiny speck, was the tower with green smudges of forest around it. The ghastly creatures, to Stan's relief, were now too tiny and far away to be seen.

"I suppose you think that was clever!" snapped Targ.

"I rescued you, didn't I?" argued Stan, a bit surprised that Targ should sound so cross.

"By stranding me on top of a mountain!" complained Targ. "I'm miles away from nowhere!"

"You are also miles away from being gobbled up," pointed out Stan. "The only other option I had was to put you back inside the tower."

"I might have been safer there," grumbled Targ.

"Never," Stan told him firmly. "Those horrible things could have chewed up the tower with you inside it."

Targ was silent for a moment, picturing this gruesome scene. "You could be right after all," he said at last. "I thank you for saving me. But what do we do now?"

"We find the Gem of Power and work out how it will help us to escape," Stan reminded him.

"How brilliant! I had quite forgotten!" scoffed Targ, getting back to his usual form again. "I mean, what do we do this minute? I can't stand perched on the edge of this precipice forever."

"You won't have to," promised Stan. "I'll think of something."

"At the speed you think," snapped Targ, "I could be here for some time."

"Then you'll just have to learn to be patient, won't you?" argued Stan. "Anyway, I'm fed up with thinking. I've had a hard day. I'm going to take a rest."

"My day has not exactly been what you'd call fun," pointed out Targ acidly. "It could have been very nasty for me if those creatures from the forest had got hold of me. And from where I'm standing now . . . "

Stan had heard enough. Targ was safe for the moment. He could stay where he was until Stan felt brainy enough to tackle his problem again. He switched off the computer and went downstairs.

"I don't know where Mum's gone. She just went out," said Stan.

Dad had come home from work to find no meal on the table and no Mum in the house. Dad was not one of those men who think that women ought to spend all day in the kitchen, but he was tired and hungry. Also, there was something he needed to talk to Mum about.

"She must have said something," grumbled Dad, poking about in the fridge for a snack.

"She just said she had to go out, and there was some cake in the cupboard," replied Stan, sitting at the kitchen table with a can of cola in front of him.

"Got it," said Dad, emerging from the cupboard with the cake in his hand. "But where she's gone to is a mystery."

Stan was hardly listening. He had mysteries of his own to solve. Targ was perched on a mountain on a faraway planet, and he was racking his brains for some way to help him. He took another drink of cola, hoping it would bubble up an idea in his mind.

"Mum's never done anything like this before." Dad was off again. "It beats me what she's . . . " He broke off as the kitchen door opened and in came Mum.

"Sorry, love," apologized Mum, looking flushed and very pleased with herself. "I was certain I'd be back in time to get your meal ready, but it took longer than I thought it would."

"What did?" asked Dad, looking mystified.

"I'll tell you when you've got a meal inside you." answered Mum, putting down her handbag and taking off her coat.

"Oh, no you won't," objected Dad, biting his way into the cake and scattering crumbs as he shook his head. "You always talk like that when you think I'm not going to like whatever it is you're going to tell me."

"You'd better like it," said Mum with a smile, "because I've already done it."

"Done what?" asked Dad, looking even more mystified than he was before.

"Found myself a part-time job," explained Mum. "One of our local dentists was advertising for a receptionist. I saw it in the paper. So I went along this afternoon and got the job. Mornings only. I start next Monday morning."

Dad sat and stared at her. So did Stan.

"It will help with the mortgage, and anyway it's something I promised myself I'd do when Stan was old enough. I'm tired of being stuck in the house all day."

Stan went on staring. So did Dad.

"That's what I like about this family," said Mum, breaking the silence at last. "You come home with a fabulous piece of news, but do they give three cheers and shout congratulations at you? They do not. They just sit there like puddings on a plate."

"Three cheers, Mum," exclaimed Stan

hastily.

"Congratulations, love," added Dad.

"That's better," beamed Mum. "Now you can both get the table ready while I produce a lightning meal."

"I've got some news too, but it's not so good," said Dad later, while they were eating. "There are going to be some changes at the steelworks. From next week I start work on the night shift."

Mum gave him a quick look. She could see that Dad was not too happy about it. Quickly she pointed out the bright side.

"Just as well, really. With me starting a day job, it will mean that there'll always be somebody here when Stan comes home from school." She glanced at Stan, saw him frowning down at his plate, and straightaway started worrying. "You won't mind, will you, Stan? You don't look too happy about it."

"No, no. Everything's fine," Stan assured her.

"Then why the face like a thunderstorm?" asked Mum.

Stan was bone weary, and both Mum and

Dad were looking at him so sympathetically that he felt he could no longer keep the secret of Targ from them. It would be a relief to share the heavy responsibility with someone else. And who better than his own family to give him all the help they could?

"I'm having terrible trouble with my computer adventure game," he told them seriously. "It's driving me crazy. I just don't know what to do for the best. There's this space traveller called Targ who is stranded . . . "

"I knew it!" growled Dad.

Stan stared at him in amazement. How could Dad possibly know about Targ.

"The hours you spend staring at that perishing computer," went on Dad. "I knew it wouldn't be long before it drove you barmy. You should be out kicking a football like other lads."

"I want you to learn about computers, you know that," added Mum. "That's why I got it for you. But Dad's quite right. You're spending far too much time working at it in your bedroom."

"Fresh air and exercise, that's what you

need," said Dad, working himself up in fine style. "So go out and get some."

"But I want you to help me," protested Stan.

"That's just what we're trying to do," explained Mum, in her most soothing voice. "Now wrap up warm and go and play in the park for a bit. It'll do you all the good in the world."

"But . . . but . . . but . . ." spluttered Stan, groping for words and not finding any.

"Never mind butting," ordered Dad. "Pop off!" Now!"

Stan gave up. He put on his anorak and left the house.

"Woof!" Stan had hardly put a foot in the park when Plato came lolloping across the grass to greet him. Stan looked around for Kathy. She was walking along behind the fringe of young trees the council were desperately trying to grow down one side of the park. Stan perked up when he saw her. Maybe she could give him a few tips about his entry for the holiday competition. Then he perked down again when he spotted the tall figure of Mark beside her. Stan would have turned away, but with Kathy waving madly at him, and Plato tugging playfully at his sleeve, he had to trot over to her.

"Can you keep a secret?" asked Kathy excitedly. "'Cos if you can, I've got something marvellous to tell you."

"Of course he can," said Mark. "Smart kid like that." He gave Stan's shoulder a playful

thump, rumpled his hair and grinned down at him. Stan nodded dumbly at Kathy, and gave Mark a disgusted look. He didn't like being used as a punchball. He was beginning to go off Mark.

"You know Mark is in the security business," went on Kathy. "Well, he's now working on the burglaries they've been having on these new estates. Exciting, isn't it?"

Stan had heard his Dad talking about these burglaries. For weeks past the newspapers had been full of stories about them. Houses on the new estates were being broken into one after another. Nothing of great value was ever stolen. The thieves seemed content to walk off with radios, toasters, video cassettes, that sort of thing. But the thefts were causing great alarm and puzzling the police.

"You'd be a dead loss in the security business," Mark told Kathy, suddenly pointing a finger at her with his thumb up in the air, as if he were holding her at gunpoint. "Can't keep a secret for five minutes, can you?"

Stan was impressed. Pretending to confront

Kathy, lean and athletic, narrow-eyed and grim, Mark certainly looked like a security agent.

"Don't you play the tough guy with me!" laughed Kathy, shaking a fist under his nose. "Anyway, you said yourself that Stan was a smart kid. He's not going to tell anyone."

"Better not, kid," growled Mark, turning his finger-gun on Stan and flipping his thumb up and down as if pretending to shoot him.

"Just watch it!" Kathy warned him. "Stan's my best friend. You do anything to him and I'll set Plato on you."

"Talking of Plato," grinned Mark, "it's about time we finished walking this dog of yours and took him home. I want to take you to the best disco in town."

"Come on, then," said Kathy, waving goodbye to Stan as they walked away across the park.

Stan was glad to see them go. Adding up his wins and losses for the day, it seemed to Stan that he had lost by a bucketful. The Raiders were going to make his life really miserable if he didn't win the travel competition and give them the free tickets. He couldn't even talk about that problem to his friend Kathy, because Secret Agent Mark, her new boyfriend, was taking up all her time. And, worst of all, the real clinker was the terrible problem of how to rescue Targ.

It was getting dark when Stan walked back to Applecombe Avenue and turned into his house. Just before he opened the door, he looked up at the stars in the sky. Blinking away, all alone in the dark, and nobody really bothered about what was going on inside them. Just like me, thought Stan, as he went inside.

"Don't you dare come into my kitchen with those muddy shoes," said Mum. "Sit down on that sheet of newspaper and take them off."

"And no more computer tonight," ordered Dad. "Your eyes are square enough already."

Stan shook his head wearily. What had he just been telling himself? Pffffff!

CHAPTER 4

At school the next day, Stan wandered out on to the playground and looked for a quiet corner where he could sit down and try to think of some way to help Targ. He was out of luck.

"Cor, look at Stan!"

"Looks like he's thinking hard."

"You can hear the wheels going round. Guddoyng! Guddoyng!"

It was the Raiders, comical as a wet Saturday afternoon.

"He's working on his entry for the holiday competition," Billy Regan explained to his cronies. "He's working really hard, 'cos he knows what'll happen to him if he doesn't win."

"I could give him a quick thump or two now, just to remind him," offered Flatnose Biggs.

"Nah," decided Regan, much to Stan's

relief. "Anyway, we've got things to do before the bell goes."

"All those kids with too much pocket-money," gloated Blinker Price, staring hungrily around the playground.

"And just waiting to hand it over," growled Flatnose Biggs.

"Let's get on with it, then," ordered Billy Regan, giving Stan an unfriendly nod and leading his gang away.

Stan hurried back into the school buildings. There would be precious little peace and quiet on the playground with the Raiders starting punch-ups all over the place. And he desperately needed to think. He went to the reception area by the main doors and stood before the big notice boards, pretending to study them and hoping to be left alone.

Suddenly the doors burst open and a small army of people came in. There was the Head, bustling about and looking important; the school caretaker, puffing and blowing and lugging some screens; and last of all, to Stan's amazement, Kathy, carrying rolls of brightly coloured travel posters.

"Stand the screens up and spread them well out," the Head told the caretaker.

"Phoo! Blah!" puffed the caretaker, getting on with the job but not looking too pleased about it.

"Use all the space you want," the Head told Kathy, waving his arms about grandly. "You will know best how to display those travel posters so as to get the attention of the children and stimulate their efforts for the competition. So I'll leave you to it. 'Bye." He gave Kathy a cheery wave and strode off down the corridor.

The caretaker stood up the last screen, glared balefully at Kathy and tramped out through the main doors. That left just Stan and Kathy, with a big bundle of posters and a packet of drawing pins.

"Hullo," said Kathy, giving Stan a pale smile. "The travel agency sent me up here. You can give me a hand, if you like."

"'Course I will," replied Stan promptly. He had given up all hope of being able to think about Targ. But maybe this was his chance to ask Kathy to give him a few tips about his entry for the competition. If he explained about his problem with the Raiders, then perhaps she wouldn't mind helping him. "I'm glad you came," he began, "because I wanted to ask you . . ."

"It's a good thing I bumped into you," interrupted Kathy, her pale smile giving way to an angry look. "I've just had the most dreadful telephone call at the travel office. If I don't tell someone about it soon I shall go mad!"

Stan blew out his cheeks hopelessly. Would nobody ever listen to what he had to say? Didn't anyone seem to care whether he had a problem or not? Anyway what was this silly old telephone call about anyway? Some twit complaining because he couldn't get hold of a packet of fish and chips on his five-day safari in West Africa?

"David telephoned to ask me if I'd go with him to a vegetarian restaurant tonight," went on Kathy. "I told him I couldn't because I was going out with Mark. Then he turned nasty." She rammed a poster showing the delights of a funtime fortnight in Florida against one of the screens and jabbed drawing pins into it as if she were stabbing somebody. Probably David.

"He said he thought I ought to know that Mark has been lying to me. He is not a security agent at all. He is just a door-to-door salesman of burglar alarms."

"How did David find that out?" gasped Stan, meeting his big surprise with round eyes and an open mouth.

"David works for an estate agent, doesn't he?" muttered Kathy, getting crosser by the minute. "He's always making house calls around the new estates. It seems that some of his clients happened to mention that they'd been called on by a burglar alarm salesman. The description fitted Mark. And of course," fumed Kathy, "David couldn't wait to pass on the bad news. I reckon he just wanted to score off Mark, just because Mark is glamorous and he's dull!"

"But Mark was the one who lied to you," Stan pointed out, wondering why on earth he was getting involved in this.

"I'll find out who's lying when I tackle Mark tonight," promised Kathy.

That seemed to finish Kathy's problem for the moment. It looked like Stan's chance to be listened to at last. But the electric bell on the wall rang itself stupid, and it was Music first period, and Miss Perkins reckoned he was a star turn in her choir. So Stan had to leave Kathy wrestling with her posters and go off to do his doh-ray-mes.

Next day was Saturday. Stan could forget about school problems and the Raiders. Kathy was obviously busy sorting out Mark and David, when she wasn't working at the travel agency, because there was no sign of her about the estate. Stan was free to concentrate on rescuing Targ. The trouble was, he couldn't think of a single idea. He was thinking hard at the kitchen table when Mum exploded.

"Here am I getting ready to go to work on Monday," she announced, in her special listen-to-me-when-I'm-talking-to-you voice, "while the two men of this house are just messing about and getting in the way."

She had bumped into the back of Stan's kitchen chair while carrying a laundry basket to the washing machine. The dirty laundry flew all over the kitchen. Stan's mug of squash toppled over and flooded the table.

"Did you call, dear?" asked Dad, hearing the rumpus, and coming in from the living room, where he had spent the last half-hour reading the paper with Mum hoovering round his feet.

"Out!" declared Mum, one arm straight up in the air like the Statue of Liberty. "The pair of you! You are barred from this house till

lunchtime. Then you can get lunch. Now go!"

Stan and Dad grabbed coats and headed for the outdoors. Dad walked Stan right across town to look at his old allotment. It was where he used to go for peace and quiet. A few of the allotment-holders he used to know were digging and raking and barrowing stuff about. Stan was bored stiff. But he could see that Dad was having a marvellous time, chatting about gardening to his old mates, so he stuck it out until it was time to go home.

Sunday was no better. Mum was still panicking about getting ready for her new job, and Dad didn't help by getting worried about how he was going to manage the change-over to working nights. Stan was as empty-headed as ever about how he was going to rescue Targ. But at least he earned himself a few good points by staying away from the computer.

On Monday afternoon after school, though, Stan couldn't stand it any longer. He was having nightmares about poor old Targ, stranded half-way up a mountain on the planet Parl. He had to do something about it. So he made himself go up to the bedroom and switch on the computer.

"Welcome back," greeted Targ. "I am, as you can see, just where you left me."

Stan did not need telling. Staring at the screen, he could see that for himself. The ★ symbol that was Targ stood perched on the edge of the precipice overlooking the forest valley where the tower stood.

"I've been thinking hard," confessed Stan, "but I just can't work out what we should do next."

"That doesn't surprise me in the slightest," crackled Targ over the computer sound system.

"If you're so clever, why don't you come up with an idea?" demanded Stan, getting a bit fed up with Targ's nose-in-the-air way of talking to him.

"I've told you before," sighed Targ, like someone patiently trying to teach a dozy puppy to beg for a biscuit. "The logic of this deadly but stupid game is so wild that it defies understanding by anything other than a low-level Earth mind like yours." He paused for a second before adding: "I seem to remember a

63

list of options you occasionally consult. Perhaps that might help."

Stan made a horror-movie face. His last session at the computer had come at the end of a difficult day. He had been worn out and fed up. That must have been why he had completely forgotten to find out what options were open to him.

"That's just what I was going to do," Stan reported hastily. "Wait a moment while I see what choices we've got."

"Better ones than last time, I hope," muttered Targ.

Stan punched the computer keys and looked hopefully at the options that flashed up on the screen:

(a) go down to the valley below
(b) thumb a lift from a passing eagle
(c) climb the mountain
(d) look for a cave to hide in.

Stan frowned. None of the options was obviously the best thing to do. But one thing was certain: he was not sending Targ back down to the valley where more of those horrible creatures might be lurking in the forests.

As for thumbing a lift from a passing eagle, that sounded silly. But maybe it was supposed to, just to put you off doing what might turn out to be the best thing.

Climbing the mountain meant following the trail as it climbed upwards. That could lead anywhere: to a safe place, or straight into the jaws of danger.

What about looking for a cave to hide in? Stan felt a prickle of excitement as he thought about it. The game's instructions had said that the Gem of Power was hidden in a secret cave. Maybe this cave was close by. They might find it, and discover the Gem of Power, and . . .

Stan shook his head. That sounded too easy to be true. It was just the sort of trick the evil dictator Vlast would play on them. They might very well find a cave, but who knows what terrible things could be waiting for them inside it? Hoping he was doing the right thing, Stan decided to take a chance on option (c). He tapped the keyboard and fixed his eyes on the screen.

"What's happening?" demanded Targ, as

his ★ symbol began moving up the trail that curved upwards around the side of the mountain.

"We're going up the mountain," explained Stan.

"I can see that," said Targ testily. "But where, and why, and . . . what's that in front of us?"

Coming into sight, just ahead of them, was a huge, fallen tree. It lay across the trail, completely blocking it. Its roots were jammed against the side of the mountain that shot straight up into the sky. Its branches jutted out over the sheer drop of the precipice on the other side of the trail. There was no way around it. They would just have to keep going and trust that the ★ symbol would just climb over it and carry on up the trail. But this it refused to do. It reached the huge trunk of the fallen tree, climbed to the top of it, and stopped.

"I can't seem to move!" complained Targ, "I'm stuck."

"Don't panic," advised Stan. "Nothing seems to be happening. You're quite safe for the moment. Let me try a few things." He tapped frantically at the computer keyboard. But nothing he did made any difference. He was about to ask Targ if he had any ideas, when a loud shriek from the computer made him jerk back his head and stare wide-eyed at the screen. The tree was tilting sideways. Targ's ★ symbol was sliding down the trunk towards the branches that hung out over the yawning drop of the precipice.

"You were wrong!" howled Targ. "Something is happening. And I'm not safe at all!"

"I'm thinking," replied Stan in a panic.

"And I'm sliding to my death!" yelled Targ. "Do anything, but do it quickly!"

Stan banged his fists on the computer desk. He had taken the option to climb the mountain, only to fall into this deadly trap. If this was just an ordinary computer game, he would have grinned ruefully and admitted that the evil dictator Vlast had beaten him this time. But this was no game as far as Targ was concerned. It was a matter of life and death. And Targ was depending on him. But what could he possibly do to help?

The idea came to him in a flash. He could switch off the computer. Targ had already explained to him that doing this would cause everything to remain freeze-fixed until he switched it on again. That way, he could win time in which to try to think of some way of rescuing Targ.

"I'm going!" shouted Targ despairingly.

The tree tilted more rapidly. Targ slid down the trunk and out on the branches hanging out over the precipice. Then the screen suddenly blanked out, as Stan dived for the button and switched the computer off.

CHAPTER 5

Later that evening, while Stan was still recovering from the shock of seeing Targ being tipped over the precipice, there was a ring on the front door-bell. Mum rushed off to answer it, excited by her first morning's work as a dentist's receptionist and unable to sit still.

"It's Kathy from next door. She wants to talk to you, Stan," announced Mum, darting upstairs to make sure that Dad was getting ready to go off for his night shift at the steelworks.

"You'll never believe what I'm going to tell you," said Kathy. "We'd better go to the park, where nobody can hear us." It sounded mysterious. Stan followed her into the park. Kathy bent down and whispered in his ear.

"It's about these burglaries on the estates. David was taken down to the police station this afternoon. They questioned him for hours.

He's worried stiff!"

"Never!" Stan couldn't believe it. The word shot out of his mouth like a rocket. Kathy shushed him frantically.

"The police have discovered that houses visited by David have afterwards been burgled," she hurried on with the bad news. "They are suspicious that there might be a connection. Everywhere he goes, there's now a police car following behind him. It's terrible! You've got to help!"

"Me!" Stan let go another word-rocket. What could he do about it? Disguise himself as David to put the police off the scent? Turn himself into a private detective and track down the real burglars? Kathy must be crazy to . . .

"You can take over the job of walking Plato in the evenings for me," explained Kathy. "I must spend all the time I can with David. He's in awful trouble, and he needs me."

"What about Mark?" asked Stan, a bit confused as to who exactly was Kathy's boyfriend at the moment.

"I am very cross with Mark for telling me a

pack of lies about himself," replied Kathy sternly. "Seeing me with David will teach him a lesson. Now will you walk Plato, starting from this evening?"

"Of course I will," said Stan promptly. "Anything to help."

Kathy shot off to be with David. Stan went back home to report.

"Good idea, walking that dog," said Dad, flinging on his coat and going off to work. "It'll get you out in the fresh air and away from that perishing computer."

"I'm glad you're so friendly with Kathy," said Mum. "She seems such a nice girl."

Stan shook his head and wondered, not for the first time, if his parents had any idea of what was happening in his world. He had tried to tell them about Targ and got nowhere. It would be useless to tell them about Kathy's problems with Mark the Mystery Man, and David's problems with the police. They'd only get worried and go on and on about it. Come to think of it, he was having just as much trouble asking Kathy about the travel competition. What did he have to do to get people to listen to him?

He asked himself the same question at school next day when he approached the Raiders with an idea that had jumped into his head when he woke up.

"Get lost!" snorted Billy Regan disdainfully, when Stan explained what he had in mind.

"Forget it!" chimed in Flatnose Biggs, taking his cue from his leader.

"Not a hope!" added Blinker Price.

"But you're always going about the new estates," said Stan. "You could keep your eyes open. Maybe you'll spot the real burglars at work and tell the police about it and become heroes!"

"Oh, har! har! har!" The Raiders fell about laughing.

"But I'm worried about these friends of mine," pleaded Stan. The Raiders screamed with mirth. Then Stan had an inspiration.

"In fact, I'm so worried," Stan told them darkly, "that I can't seem to concentrate on my holiday competition entry. If you did something to help, then I wouldn't be so

worried, and I'd have a better chance of winning."

Regan abruptly stopped laughing. His henchmen, copying his every move as always, suddenly went serious and frowned at Stan.

"You know what I think?" growled Regan, prodding Stan in the chest and looking nasty. "I think you're making up these stories just in case you write a rotten entry and don't win us those free holiday tickets."

"That's what he's doing, all right," agreed Flatnose.

"No doubt about it," put in Blinker.

"Well, it won't work," declared Regan menacingly. "You'll get that entry in by the end of the week, and it will win the competition, or else . . . " The threat was rounded off by three fists being shoved under Stan's nose. The Raiders stalked away. Stan looked helplessly at the sky. It was no help. Neither was Mr Bartlett in that afternoon's English lesson.

"Please, sir," said Stan, when Mr Bartlett had handed out the period assignments and was settling himself comfortably in the chair behind his desk to begin filling in an application form for a job in a posh school.

"Is that leaky radiator making funny noises again?" asked Mr Bartlett sarcastically. "No, it's not. It's Stanley Wheeler. Speak lad, and make it brief."

"About the holiday competition," Stan ploughed on. "What sort of things do you think they want us to write? I mean, can you give us any tips?" After his little chat with the Raiders, Stan was looking for all the help he could get. "What I mean is," Stan struggled to make himself clear, "you're our English teacher, and you're supposed to help us, and winning this competition could be very important to me — I mean, all of us."

"Get out your dictionaries!" barked Mr Bartlett, ignoring Stan and addressing the entire form. "Now look up the word 'nitwit'. Come on, come on, don't take all day!"

There was a mad rustling of pages. Then Eileen Parks, a thin, freckled-faced girl with pigtails stuck up a hand.

"Please, sir, 'nitwit' means 'a person of little intelligence'."

75

"Right. Now look up the word 'buffoon'," ordered Mr Bartlett.

"It means 'wag, jester or mocker'," announced Eileen Parks, obviously a wizard with a dictionary, and getting there first again.

"After that little exercise," declared Mr Bartlett, looking more like a hungry vulture than ever, "everyone will understand what I'm going to say now. Stanley Wheeler," giving Stan a filthy look, "you are either a nitwit or a buffoon. When I have decided which, I shall punish you accordingly. Now all of you, get on with your work!"

Stan gave up. He decided, in that dark moment, that he might never try to tell the world anything ever again.

Back home after school, Stan was amazed to find that nobody wanted him to stay away from the computer, or kick a football, or get some fresh air, or anything. Mum had come home very happy with her second day as a dentist's receptionist. Dad had spent a rotten day trying to get some sleep, and was now not looking forward at all to his second night-shift.

"I'll never get used to it, love," he told Mum. "It's not natural, working all night and sleeping all day."

"You'll get used to it," Mum tried to calm him down. "There's one of your gardening programmes on the telly early this evening. You'll have plenty of time to watch it."

"That's about as close as I'll ever get to a garden again," grumbled Dad.

"Finished your meal, Stan?" said Mum. "Then why don't you go upstairs to your computer? Dad could do with a bit of peace and quiet."

Stan went, thinking he could do with a bit of peace and quiet himself. He had left Targ dangling over a precipice. He spent a moment working out exactly what he was going to do about it. Then he switched on. The computer screen flashed into life, showing the ★ symbol that was Targ bobbing wildly about in the branches of the tree which was tilting sideways over the abyss. Stan hammered at the keyboard. The action froze as the screen displayed a list of options:

(a) Give up and fall to your death

77

(b) Learn to fly

(c) Go to the roots of your trouble.

Stan blinked. The first two choices were ridiculous. The last was mysterious, but it was obviously the one to go for. He hesitated only a moment before selecting option (c).

At once, the tree stopped tilting. Stan was able to move Targ up from the branches and back on to the main trunk of the tree. Then he noticed that the roots of the tree, as it tilted upwards, had ripped open what looked like the entrance to a huge cave in the side of the mountain. He had done it! He had gone to the tree-roots of his trouble and saved Targ. Better still, thought Stan jubilantly, he had discovered the secret cave holding the Gem of Power. He was a genius!

"I think not," said Targ, sounding breathless after his narrow escape. "This is a very strange cave. I don't like it at all."

Stan could see what he meant. The cave seemed to be swallowing them up. They were hurtling down a narrow, winding tunnel. It was like the ghost train at a funfair. But this was no funfair, and Stan was really scared.

Suddenly the speck of light grew into a blaze of harsh sunlight, and they stopped abruptly. In front of them was a deep ravine. Across it lay a rope bridge with wooden slats for footholds. But the ropes were frayed and the wood was rotten. So how were they going to cross it?

"We can't just stay here," crackled Targ. "Vlast could destroy me where I stand."

"Then you'll just have to cross the bridge," urged Stan, beginning to feel scared at what might happen, but even more scared of Vlast.

Targ moved forward on to the bridge and began to cross it. The wooden slats creaked and crumbled as he went. Stan watched him, hardly daring to breathe. The computer's sound system began to give out a high-pitched, ghostly call. Stan shook his head and tried not to listen. The sound grew louder and more threatening, until Stan realized it was not the computer at all. It was his mother's voice calling from downstairs.

"Have you forgotten what you promised Kathy? It's time for you to take Plato for his walk." She must have been calling for some time, because she now started to climb the stairs.

"I'm fed up with shouting. I'm coming to get you!"

Stan panicked. He couldn't let anyone come near the computer. Not with Targ starting to cross the ravine. Anything could go wrong.

"I'm coming, I'm coming!" he yelled, rushing out of the bedroom and slamming the door behind him.

But forgetting to switch off the computer.

And not until the following day after school did Stan find out what amazing things were now going to happen.

CHAPTER 6

"But how did you do it?"

Stan asked the question after rushing home from school next day, going to the computer and finding it still switched on. The screen now showed him Targ, safely across the bridge, on the other side of the ravine, standing in front of a wide cave. In the mouth of the cave, smothered in ivy, was a flat rock holding an enormous blue gemstone that gave off rays of brilliant light.

"Quite simple," said Targ modestly. "When you left the computer switched on overnight, I found I could draw power from your mains electricity supply. I used this power to return myself temporarily to pure energy status, and cross the ravine in particle form. On the other side of the bridge was the cave we have been seeking. You are now looking at the Gem of Power."

"Then we've won!" exulted Stan, baffled by Targ's explanation, but happy all the same.

"Not quite," Targ reminded him. "We still have to work out how the Gem of Power can help us to escape. I shall need to examine it carefully. Let's go closer."

That was a mistake. As soon as Targ moved towards the rock on which the Gem of Power stood, the ivy leaves that smothered it began to detach themselves one by one and zoom towards him like dagger-shaped rockets. It was a deadly hail that could destroy him in an instant, but even worse was to follow. While still hurling their death-leaves at Targ, the long ivy-branches began untwining from the rock and slithering towards him like serpents. As they came, they grew slanted eyes and fang-lined jaws.

"Help!" screeched Targ.

Stan felt as if he had fallen into a nightmare. Staring at the screen in horrible fascination, he tapped desperately at the keyboard, dodging the ★ symbol this way and that as the monsters repeatedly attacked. But try as he might, Stan knew that he could never move Targ about quickly enough to avoid all the threats to his life.

He forced himself to be braver than he ever thought he could be. Taking a final, desperate gamble, he abandoned the keys which moved the ★ symbol about the screen, and reached instead for the laser-gun firing key. While the dagger-shaped rockets roared down, and the serpents closed in on Targ, Stan jabbed again and again at the laser-gun key. It was a furious battle, but Stan, fighting for Targ's life and determined not to be beaten, wiped out the last rocket and final writhing serpent.

"Thank you once again," said Targ. "I really don't know where I'd be without you. You're a wonderful help to me. Now let's take a look at the Gem of Power and find out how it can help us to escape."

Stan did not have Targ's powers of recovery. He slumped back in his chair, worn out by his efforts. It was all beginning to be a bit too much for him to cope with. What with Targ, and the Raiders, and Kathy's problems, he felt overwhelmed, just like Targ had felt a few moments before. Stan sat up at the thought.

He had been a wonderful help to Targ. Why couldn't Targ be a wonderful help to him?

"Forget about the Gem of Power, just for the moment," he told Targ. "I desperately need your advice."

"I'm not sure I can help you with Earth problems," warned Targ. "But I'll be only too happy to try."

Stan's fingers flew over the keyboard. He told Targ about the burglaries, and David's troubles with the police, and how Kathy was worrying about him. He asked what was the best thing he could do to help.

"Catch the real burglar," answered Targ promptly.

"And just how am I supposed to do that?" demanded Stan.

Targ thought about it for a microsecond, then: "Find the person who has the most to gain from the burglaries," he advised. "Work out his method of operation, then lay a trap for him. Now please can I examine the Gem of Power before Vlast finds out where we are?"

"Just one more thing," pleaded Stan, and he told Targ how he just had to win the holiday competition to save himself from the Raiders.

"What is a holiday?" Targ was completely puzzled. "And why have a competition? You Earth dwellers go about things in a very funny way, if you ask me."

"I'm asking how I can win it," Stan reminded him sharply.

"Well, how do I know?" protested Targ. "Anyway, you're supposed to write the entry yourself, without getting help from anyone else."

"I mustn't ask my parents to help me," Stan pointed out. "They didn't say anything about not getting advice from beings from outer space."

Targ was silent for at least four microseconds, which showed how difficult he was finding the problem.

"Be yourself and tell the truth," he said at last.

"Oh, thanks a lot!" replied Stan sarcastically. "That's supposed to win me the competition, is it?"

"I can't think of anything else that will," was Targ's last word on the matter. "Now please leave me in peace to study the Gem of Power."

Stan switched off the computer and went downstairs. Targ was going to be busy, and he had a lot to think about. Dad was in the kitchen, giving Mum a lot to think about.

"I can't get used to sleeping in the daytime," he was telling her. "So I went out for a walk this afternoon. I went past the Job Centre, and there it was in the window."

"What was?" asked Mum, wondering what he was talking about.

"A card advertising a job in the Council Parks Department," explained Dad excitedly. "There and then I decided to stop worrying about being made redundant at the steelworks. I raced round to the Town Hall and saw the bloke in charge. By the time I'd finished telling him what a smashing gardener I was, I'd got the job. I start in two weeks. Yippee!"

"Not such good money, though, But we'll manage somehow," smiled Mum. But Stan could tell from her face that she was beginning to wonder if it had been such a good idea to move her family into the new house.

"I got the idea from watching a movie on television," said Stan, fibbing his head off. "All we have to do is work out who gains most from these burglaries. Then set a trap for him."

Leaving Mum and Dad to their chat, he had sprinted round to Kathy's house and got her to telephone David. Now they were sitting in David's car, where nobody could overhear them. Stan was sitting beside Plato on the back seat.

"Daft idea!" grumbled Kathy. "The one who gains is the burglar when he makes off with the loot. So where does that get us?"

"Wait a minute." David was thinking hard. His eyes brightened as if he had thought of something really good. Then he looked doubtfully at Kathy. "You're not going to like this idea, but . . . "

"Go on," Stan urged him.

". . . but maybe the one who gains most is Mark," suggested David. "He sells burglar alarms doesn't he? These burglaries must be good for his business."

"You're just saying that because you're jealous!" stormed Kathy. "You've no right to make such accusations, just because you don't like me going out with Mark! I was feeling really sorry for you, David. Now I'm beginning to think I was wasting my time!"

Plato gave a threatening growl. When Kathy got angry, Plato got angry too. Stan shifted nervously away from him.

"But it makes sense," persisted David stubbornly. "The burglar only steals small articles. Mark could easily take them away in his car."

"I've heard enough of this nonsense!" declared Kathy, jumping out of the car and hauling Plato from the back seat. "I may never speak to either of you two again!" She walked off homewards, leaving Stan and David gazing open-mouthed after her.

"I still think I'm right," muttered David rebelliously. "What do you think?"

Stan tried to imagine what Targ would say. "Mark is the only suspect we've got," he said at last. "But how does he go about these burglaries?"

"Let's see." David chewed his thumb, thinking furiously. "He goes to a new estate and starts knocking on doors, telling people how fantastic his burglar alarms are. That gives him a chance to find out which house is likely to be empty during the evening. Then he comes back after dark and robs the house. Next day he's back on the estate selling burglar alarms like mad to all the scared householders. All we have to do is find out which estate he's working on at the moment, and then set a trap for him."

"What kind of trap?" asked Stan. He wasn't at all sure that David was right. But there was no harm in trying out the idea.

"The kind that can't fail," decided David, getting really excited as he told Stan what he had in mind.

Later that night, before going to bed, Stan sat down at the kitchen table with a ball-point pen and a writing pad. His head was still buzzing with the events of the day, but he couldn't put off writing his holiday entry any longer. Usually, when Stan had to write something at school, he stared at the classroom wall until an idea struggled into his brain and then scrawled it down as fast as he could before he could forget it. Mr Bartlett would go berserk about his handwriting, but at least the job was done. But this was different. His holiday entry just had to be good enough to win the competition, or else his life wouldn't be worth living.

"I didn't know you could write," joked Dad, coming in from the living room where he and Mum were watching television. "I thought you did everything on that computer of yours.

Except take a bath, of course!"

He walked out with the biscuit tin. Stan rolled his eyes to the ceiling and tried to fix his mind on his idea of the perfect holiday. "Be yourself and tell the truth," had been Targ's advice. Some help. All the same, mused Stan, there might be something in it. Lots of kids would be making up stories about the kind of holidays you see advertised on television. What if he wrote about holidays in his own way — a way that nobody else would ever think of? Perhaps . . .

"Bit late to be doing your homework, isn't it?" said Mum, walking in from the living room to make a cup of tea. "Your Dad will want a meal before he goes to work tonight, so don't be mortally offended if you have to shift yourself to one end of the table soon."

She clattered cups, rattled spoons, sloshed water, picked up the tray and strolled out, giving him a beaming smile. Stan suddenly felt like someone whose half-finished jigsaw puzzle had been scattered all over the floor. He scowled at the writing paper trying to fit his thoughts together again. What he was going to

write might not be the poshest entry in the competition. But at least it would be his own, and it would be truthful.

"My perfect holiday," he began, "would be one where Mum and Dad could forget all their worries. I would take them to . . . "

And from there on, writing it was no trouble at all.

CHAPTER 7

"Disaster!" Targ shrieked the word through the computer's sound system as soon as Stan switched on next day after school. Stan was petrified. He had left Targ safe in the secret cave and trying to work out how the Gem of Power could help them escape. Now he was shouting his head off. What had gone wrong?

"The evil dictator Vlast is about to destroy us!" yelled Targ.

"But he can't do that," protested Stan. "We've won the game. It isn't fair."

"What makes you think Vlast has to be fair? He's an evil dictator, isn't he?" snapped Targ. "At this very moment, from his mountain fortress, he is preparing to dispatch a force of combat craft armed with ultimate destructive weapons. He intends to smash the Gem of Power into a million fragments. This may well destroy the planet Parl. But Vlast doesn't care.

He refuses to be beaten. He would rather die first."

"How did you find all this out?" asked Stan, feeling the back of his neck go cold with fear.

"While examining the Gem of Power, I found that it was a controllable source of mighty energy," explained Targ hurriedly. "So I used it to construct a fourth-level radar system that would locate and scan anything on the planet. It told me that Vlast's combat craft were about to be launched, their destination and their weaponry."

Stan suddenly had a brilliant idea. "Why don't you use the Gem of Power to make a defensive weapon to shield you from Vlast's combat craft?" he suggested.

"Not possible," confessed Targ, in a voice as cold as ice. "Thinking, like you, that we had won the game, I had already committed the total energy output of the Gem of Power to the construction of a space craft that would enable me to return to my planet Karothan. Then I remembered that Vlast was supposed to be planning a gruesome death for us. This made me think that he might yet try to cheat us. So I withdrew just enough energy to make the fourth-level radar.''

"Well, draw out some more energy," replied Stan impatiently.

"Never!" declared Targ. "I need every particle of energy for my space craft. Without it, I shall be stranded here forever."

Stan could see a flaw in Targ's reasoning. "But if Vlast destroys the Gem of Power, you'll be stranded anyway," he argued. "You've got to defend yourself."

"Not if I have you to defend me," pointed out Targ.

"Me?" Stan was stunned. "You're going to rely on me?"

"Why not?" said Targ. "You have been a good friend to me. I trust you in all things. You will not let me down now."

It was an awesome responsibility. Stan was scared stiff. What helped to stiffen his courage was the knowledge that Targ, in the face of ultimate danger, trusted him. It was a proud feeling. Stan paused a moment, frantically trying to think of the best thing to do. Then he rattled the keyboard. It was a forlorn hope, but maybe there was a game option which would allow him to counter Vlast's treacherous move. The choices that flashed up on the screen were not helpful:

(a) Use any resource you have discovered during the game

(b) Escape by the Gem of Power, if you can

(c) Destroy the attacking combat craft.

Stan shook his head helplessly. Why couldn't Targ have found a cleverer person to defend him? Then he gave himself a mental kick in the trousers. It was no good brooding like that. He would just have to do the best he could. And he had better be right. He stared at the options and did some high-speed thinking.

Option (a) was no good. It was just another way of saying "You're on your own". As for escaping by the Gem of Power, Targ was already doing that; but it would take time, and Vlast would be launching his attack at any moment. What about using his laser-gun key to try and shoot down Vlast's combat craft? Stan made a horror-comic face. He had been absolutely shattered after his battle with the monsters guarding the cave of the Gem of

Power. He couldn't see himself being skilful enough to deal with hordes of Vlast's speed-of-light combat craft. He stared at option (a) again.

"Use any resource . . . " Stan sent his mind chasing over the many problems he and Targ had faced together. It came back to him empty-handed. He could recall nothing of any use to him now. Stan banged the computer desk in a temper. Why did he have to be lumbered with this responsibility? Why couldn't he be another person, in some other place . . . ?

He stopped ranting as a super idea, swift and brilliant as lightning, flashed into his brain. Some other place . . . that was it! Remember the time-and-space maze surrounding the tower where their adventures had begun? Remember how he had got rid of it by relocating it around a distant swamp on the planet Parl? That was a resource he had discovered during the game. So why couldn't he use it now?

Stan's flying fingers selected option (a). The computer screen immediately confronted him

with: "Give your command." Stan gave it, typing in as fast as he could: "Relocate time-and-space maze around Vlast's mountain fortress to lock up forever the evil dictator and all his forces."

A dazzle of whirling patterns filled the screen. Then it cleared, to show Targ's ★ symbol, bright and steady, in the cave of the Gem of Power.

"Astonishing!" cried Targ's voice. "My fourth-level radar probe displays a matter-vacuum where Vlast's mountain fortress stood. No Vlast. No combat craft. Nothing!" And when Stan had explained his master-stroke: "Wonderful! I had no idea that you Earth dwellers could be so clever!" Coming from Targ, this was a real compliment. Stan felt flushed with pride. If a super-brain like Targ though he was clever, then . . .

"In that case, you wouldn't agree that I was a nitwit or a buffon, would you?" asked Stan, remembering resentfully the names that Mr Bartlett had called him.

"Whoever called you that is himself a nitwitted buffon!" replied Targ promptly.

"You have quite changed my mind about Earth people. When I get back to Karothan I shall give the planet Earth a quite favourable report. Which reminds me — I have much work to do. There is the space craft to construct and my navigational courses to be worked out. Perhaps it would be best if you switched off the computer now and left me to get on with it."

"You'll not go without saying goodbye?" said Stan anxiously.

"Of course not," Targ assured him. "I shall say a final thank-you before I go."

Satisfied that they would be talking again, and happy that Targ would be safe while he worked on his tasks, Stan switched off the computer. There was a choc-ice in the fridge. He felt he had earned it. He had defeated the evil dictator Vlast and led Targ safely to the Gem of Power. Nothing could go wrong now . . . could it?

"This has got to be the right house. Go on, bang the door," growled Billy Regan.

The Raiders had come looking for Stan. They had a big and very nasty surprise for him.

Flatnose Biggs banged the door like a drum. Blinker Price played tunes on the doorbell.

Curled up in an armchair in the living room, Stan groaned at the interruption. The choc-ice had gone down nicely. Now he was enjoying his favourite television cartoon show. Why didn't Mum or Dad answer the door? Then he remembered. Dad had gone into town to meet Mum from the dentist's and go shopping for the overalls and boots he would need for his new job with the Parks Department.

"Surprise, surprise!" hooted the Raiders when Stan opened the door, blinking at them in astonishment.

"We've been thinking about you, Stan," rasped Regan. "Ever since that last chat we had in the playground."

"Yeh. You reckoned you were worried about these burglaries and those friends of yours," chimed in Blinker.

"Couldn't get your mind on the job of writing the competition entry," sniggered Flatnose.

"So we thought we'd come up and give you a hand," explained Regan, with a menacing look on his face.

Stan was getting alarmed. With nobody in the house he was going to have to face the Raiders alone. He stared up and down the avenue. There was a removal van parked outside one of the newly completed houses, where a family was obviously moving in. But apart from that the avenue was empty.

"Grab him!" ordered Regan.

Flatnose grabbed one of Stan's arms and Blinker fastened on to the other, as two removal men jumped out of their van and flung open the back doors to begin lugging furniture. Stan opened his mouth to yell for help. The yell changed into an anguished gasp as Regan kicked him painfully on the shin. The removal men glanced across at them, grinned at what they thought was a bunch of kids larking about and got on with their work. The Raiders bundled Stan inside the house and shut the front door.

"Listen, ratbag," hissed Regan. "Go and tell your Mum and Dad that some school chums have come to play games. Then show us where your computer is." He saw Stan hesitate and guessed why. "Mum and Dad not in, are they? Well isn't that just great. Now we can play all the games we want. Like wrecking the kitchen for a start."

"And kicking in the telly!" chuckled Flatnose.

"Throw washing powder all over the carpets!" suggested Blinker.

Stan was horrified. The Raiders were crazy

enough to do all those things. He couldn't imagine why they wanted to see his computer, but if that's what it took to keep them quiet . . .

"The computer's upstairs in my bedroom," he told them hurriedly. "Come on. I'll show you."

They trooped up to the bedroom. The Raiders made him show them everything — the computer and every bit of software that he had, even the floppy disk holding the Gem of Power game that they made him take out of the machine. They were as thick as he had always imagined them to be. The computer system meant nothing to them at all. But he didn't trust them. He wanted them out of the house as fast as possible.

"I've decided not to use the computer for the competition after all," he told them. "I've written the entry myself. It'll be better that way."

"Do it any way you like," said Regan, grinning like a sabre-toothed tiger. "We're just here to be helpful."

"What do you mean?" asked Stan warily.

Regan scooped up every floppy disk in sight, including the one with the Gem of Power game on it.

"Get that competition entry in by the end of the week and make sure it wins!" snarled Regan. "To help you keep your mind on the job we'll keep all these. If you try anything funny, or get ideas about double-crossing us, we'll destroy the lot of them."

Clutching the floppy disks, and jerking his head to order his cronies to follow him, Regan turned and went. The Raiders barged downstairs and out through the front door.

"But you can't — you mustn't — you don't understand!" shouted Stan. He ran frantically after them and chased them down the avenue.

"Har! Har! Har!" jeered the Raiders, scuttling across the park. Well used to being chased by irate shopkeepers, arcade owners and the odd policeman, the Raiders left Stan standing.

"Come back — please!" He let out a last despairing screech. But it was useless. The Raiders were gone.

Stan turned back to the house feeling like

death. The worst disaster he could ever have imagined had just happened to him. He had rescued Targ from the perils of the planet Parl only to have him captured on Earth by a gang of toughies. The Raiders couldn't be trusted not to do anything stupid. Stan couldn't be certain that his entry would win the competition. He might never be able to get back the disk holding the Gem of Power adventure.

All along, Targ had trusted Stan with his life. And now, just when things were looking good, he had failed miserably. Targ could die, or be stranded in limbo for ever, he told himself miserably, and there was nothing, absolutely nothing, he could do about it.

CHAPTER 8

"I'm not talking to you, Stanley Wheeler! You're no friend of mine!" Kathy Day glared at Stan and stormed past him. She was on her way to the park with Plato. Stan was trudging back home up the avenue, miserable and shattered after the Raider robbery.

"And you can forget about taking Plato for walks. I wouldn't trust my dog to a boy like you!"

"But w-what did I do?" stammered Stan, thunderstruck.

"Oh, nothing much," snapped Kathy, heels clicking on the pavement as she went on her way. "Just getting together with that fool David to accuse Mark of being a burglar, that's all!"

With everything he had on his mind, it took Stan a moment to recall the scene in David's car when Kathy had angrily walked out on the pair of them. She was clearly still furious. Stan ran after her.

"There's something much more important I've got to talk to you about," he said urgently.

"Huh!" Kathy towed Plato on to the park and turned him loose.

"You've got to listen to me!" urged Stan.

"Why should I?" demanded Kathy icily.

"Because I'm in terrible trouble, and nobody else in the world will listen to me!" said Stan, the words coming tumbling out in a mad rush.

Kathy gave him a curious look. She had never seen Stan like this before. He was dead serious, and panic-stricken.

"It's all happening on my computer," began Stan. He went on to tell Kathy everything — how Targ, travelling across the galaxy, had landed by accident in his computer adventure game, how he had guided Targ through many dangers to the Gem of Power, and, worst of all, how the Raiders had stolen his computer disks. "I've got to get them back," finished Stan desperately, "or Targ will be lost forever!"

Kathy stared at him, not saying a word.

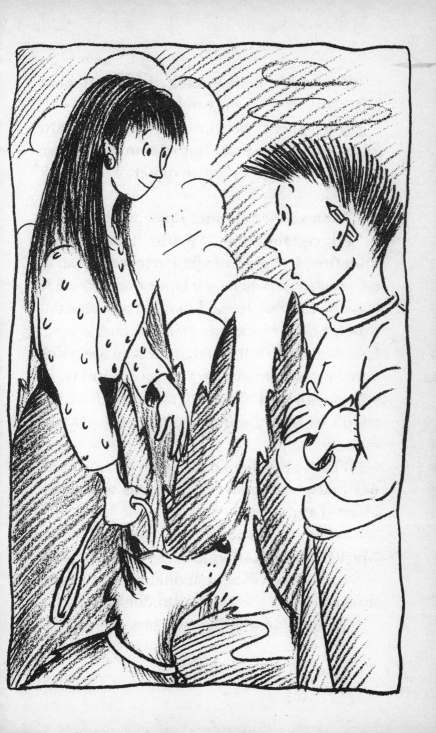

"You don't believe me!" burst out Stan bitterly. "I knew you wouldn't."

Kathy shook her head. "I never heard anything so amazing. But of course I believe you. You wouldn't be so upset if it wasn't true."

"Then you'll help me?" pleaded Stan.

"I'll certainly try," Kathy assured him. "But first, I've got a confession to make. David telephoned me when I got home from work. He was very excited. He said that he had found out which house Mark was going to burgle next. He asked me to tell you that the trap was going to be sprung tonight." Kathy looked guilty. "I was so mad with him that I slammed down the telephone. And I was not going to give you the message."

"That's all right. You have now," said Stan, not really caring because he was so worried about Targ.

"What's this trap you're going to set for Mark?" asked Kathy, looking worried too.

Stan told her. Kathy smouldered a bit as she listened. Then she went all thoughtful.

"You two are not the only ones who can set

traps," she muttered at last. "I think I know a way to get your computer disks back from the Raiders. But you'll have to do a bit of acting to persuade them to fall into the trap. Think you can do that?"

Stan nodded madly. "I'll do anything," he vowed.

Kathy called Plato and they all rushed back to Kathy's house. She telephoned David, asked him for the address of the house that Mark was supposed to be burgling, and finished up by telling him to bring his car round to her house that evening. "We're all coming with you," she told David firmly. "I am determined once and for all to have Mark cleared or proved guilty. And I want to be there when it happens!"

She put down the phone and turned to Stan, "There's not much time, so you'll have to hurry. Go and find the Raiders. Tell them to meet you tonight at the address I've written down on this piece of paper. They must bring the computer disks with them. When they hand over the disks, you will give them your competition entry. Plato and I will be there to

113

make sure they don't try anything funny."

"But how can we be sure they'll come?" asked Stan nervously.

"Say that you're going to prove to them that your entry is bound to win the competition. That'll fetch them," replied Kathy confidently.

"How am I going to do that?" said Stan, wondering what on earth she was talking about.

"You'll see when the time comes," was all Kathy would tell him. "Just act desperate and convince them they've got to come. Now hurry!"

Stan dashed home and got out his bike. If there was one place he could be certain of finding the Raiders it was the amusement arcade in the middle of town. They spent all their spare cash and most of their spare time there. Stan tore into town, parked his bike and pushed his way into the crowded arcade.

"Sounds funny to me," grunted Regan suspiciously, when Stan delivered the message and address that Kathy had given him.

"Very dodgy," agreed Blinker. "That

estate's right up the top of town."

"Why don't I just thump him and chuck him out?" suggested Flatnose.

Stan remembered Kathy's advice and acted desperate. "You've got to come," he said breathlessly. "I dare not meet you any closer to home. I'll get into real trouble if my parents find out that all my computer disks have gone."

"Too bad!" scoffed Flatnose.

"Boo-hoo! You've got me crying my eyes out!" jeered Blinker.

"Shut-up!" growled Regan, reducing his henchmen to instant silence, and glowering at Stan. "Now what's all this garbage about proving to us that your entry is going to win?"

"You'll see when you get there. Honest!" swore Stan, acting as desperate as he possibly could.

"Nine o'clock, and you'd better be there," threatened Regan.

"No, it's got to be eight o'clock," insisted Stan. "My parents don't like me to be out too late."

Regan gave him a silent sneer. "Right. You

can throw him out now," he ordered Flatnose and Blinker.

And they did.

That evening, when it was getting dark, Stan sat nervously behind the steering wheel of David's car. Kathy and Plato were in the back seat. David was standing in a telephone kiosk ahead of them down the street.

Headlights blazed as a car swung into the street, swept past them, braked in a squeal of tyres at the cross-roads and roared away. Stan shot up, then slumped back in his seat. It was exhausting being a private eye. How many more times would he have to go rigid with excitement as a car appeared, only to glare disappointedly after it as it vanished again? How much longer would they have to wait? Why hadn't anybody shown up? Had something gone wrong? He jumped when Kathy suddenly broke the silence.

"I don't believe it?" she cried. "Look at that!"

Stan stared through the side window. A car was cruising slowly past them. Unlike David's

116

nondescript model, this was a flash sports car. It was Mark's. They watched it go a short way down the street and pull up outside a darkened house, whose occupants had obviously gone out for the evening. A man climbed out and softly shut the car door. He was dressed like a shadow — black ski hood, black sweater and slacks. They froze as he looked back at David's parked car, then breathed again as, apparently satisfied it was no threat, he darted towards the house.

Stan waited for a few moments, then reached for the controls and blinked the sidelights of David's car — once, twice. Watching from the telephone kiosk, David picked up the signal. He lifted the receiver and telephoned the police with an urgent message. The plan was working brilliantly. Then it all went wrong.

"Somebody else is coming!" hissed Kathy, shoving Plato to one side so that Stan could look through the rear window.

A group of noisy youngsters were swaggering down the pavement. They did Tarzan leaps at every street light they passed. "Rah, rah, rah!" they chanted, prancing about like dervishes. It was the Raiders, keeping their appointment with Stan.

"Oh no!" moaned Stan. They had fixed the meeting with the Raiders for eight o'clock because they didn't think the burglar would show up till later. They had guessed wrongly. The noisy Raiders might scare off the burglar before the police could get there. "This is total disaster!" groaned Stan.

"There's still a chance," urged Kathy. "But

it all depends on you. You've got to shut them up. Can you remember what you've got to do?''

Stan nodded, thrilled and scared at the same time. He got out of the car and stood on the pavement where the Raiders could see him.

"It's swap time, Stan," said Regan, barging up to him. "Let's have your competition entry, and no funny business."

Stan reached into his anorak, took out the envelope containing his competition entry and handed it over. "Now what about my computer disks?" he demanded.

"Slow down, Stan," growled Regan, tucking Stan's envelope inside his shirt. "You're forgetting something. How about proving to us that your entry is bound to win? That was the deal, remember?"

"Take a look behind you," said Stan.

The Raiders whipped round. Kathy had got out of the car and was standing on the edge of a pool of darkness, just where the Raiders could see her face in the glow of the street light.

"Cor!" breathed Flatnose. "It's her from the travel agency."

"The one who put up those posters in school!" croaked Blinker.

"She lives next door to me. She's my best friend," explained Stan.

"Cle-he-ver!" grunted Regan approvingly, jumping to the wrong conclusion that everyone was as big a cheat as he was. "You've got more brains than I thought. With her on your side, this entry has just got to win! Very smart, Stan. We'll be off, then. Cheers!"

Stan stuck out a hand. "My computer disks," he reminded Regan.

"Pricey things," grinned Regan. "I can sell them for real money."

"But you promised to hand them over," insisted Stan, really alarmed that Regan was about to double-cross him.

"So I'm a liar. So what?" snarled Regan, thumping a fist into Stan's chest. "Come on, you lot. Scarper!" he shouted.

The Raiders hurtled back down the pavement towards Kathy, who stepped from her pool of darkness with Plato beside her. Plato gave a rumbling growl. The Raiders stopped, scared out of their wits.

Just then a police car with flashing blue lights roared into the street and braked to a stop when David, waiting on the pavement, waved it down. The Raiders, terrified by this display of force, and thinking that the police had come to pick them up, thrust the computer disks and the competition entry into Kathy's hands and raced off into the darkness.

Stan stood beside Kathy and watched as the police went into the house and came out shortly afterwards with the black-clad burglar. The man had taken off his black ski hood. They could see his face clearly. It was Mark. He was put into the police car and driven away.

"I'm sorry it had to turn out like this," said David to Kathy, when he had finished talking to the policeman who had remained behind to keep an eye on the house until the occupants returned.

"I'm not," said Kathy. "You stopped me making a fool of myself. And I'm sorry for all the rotten things I said to you."

"Can we go home now?" begged Stan. Kathy and David had a lot they seemed to want to say to each other, and he didn't want to be bored having to listen.

Besides, he had far more important things to do. He had the computer disks safely tucked away in his anorak. But had the Raiders damaged them. Was Targ still alive? He could hardly wait to get home to find out.

CHAPTER 9

"Stop! Take another step and I'll spread you all over the wallpaper!"

Stan had rushed into the house and was dashing upstairs. The sudden yell halted him half-way. It was Mum, and she was not pleased.

"I want to know where you've been, and what you've been doing, and why it's taken you so long to get home," she went on, sounding like the Flying Squad checking out a bank robbery.

Stan reluctantly came downstairs and followed her into the kitchen where Dad was having a last cup of tea before his night shift.

"I had to go out. It was important." Stan hesitated before saying any more. He had tried once to tell them about his troubles. Now he had even more to tell, and he didn't know where to begin. "I've been with Kathy and her

123

boyfriend," he said at last.

Mum relaxed. "That's all right then. But it's not like you to miss a meal. I've saved something for you, so sit down and tuck in. We've got news for you." When Mum was bubbling like this it was no good arguing with her. Stan slipped off his anorak and got on with his meal.

"That computer of yours," said Mum.

Stan nearly choked on a chunk of sausage.

Something had happened to his computer while he was out. This was total disaster! Dad thumped him on the back and made him spill his orange juice. Stan coughed and panicked at the same time.

"Best thing that ever happened to us," continued Mum, beaming brightly. "The dentist I work for has decided to expand the practice, and take on a partner, and computerize all his records. When I told him how I'd helped you to learn how to use your computer, he offered to give me a full-time receptionist's job and send me on a training course. What do you think about that, then?"

Red-faced and watery-eyed after his choking fit, Stan could only nod his head madly and give her a big smile.

"He looks like Dracula on a bad day," grinned Dad.

"Knowing my family," declared Mum, "that is the closest I'll get to hearing them telling me what a genius I am."

"'Course you are," said Dad. "Our money troubles are as good as over, and I'm about to kiss the steelworks goodbye and start gardening for a living. And it's all down to you."

"Great news, Mum," Stan managed to say at last. "You're the best ever."

"For that you get a pudding," laughed Mum, slapping it down in front of him.

Dad went off to work. Mum relaxed in front of the television. Stan swallowed the last of his pudding, grabbed the computer disks from his anorak and sprinted up to his bedroom. He switched on the computer. It made the usual beeping, humming noises while it warmed up. Stan put in the Gem of Power disk, crossed his fingers, held his breath and prayed that everything was all right.

The screen flooded with bright colours. The secret cave of the Gem of Power seemed to have got much bigger. The Gem itself, lying on its rock slab, was throbbing and pulsating as if charged with tremendous energy. In the centre of the cave stood a massive rocket launcher with a space capsule perched on its tip. Targ's ★ symbol, brighter and larger than ever, was beside it.

"Are you all right?" typed in Stan.

Everything looked good, but he had to be sure.

"Why shouldn't I be?" asked Targ, a little impatiently Stan thought.

"I could tell you, but it would take too long," replied Stan. "How are you getting on?"

"I'm on the point of getting off," said Targ. And the computer sound system gave out a tinny chuckle. Targ had made a joke — his first ever. Not brilliant, reckoned Stan, but at least he was trying. "What I mean is," went on Targ, "I am ready to depart for my home planet of Karothan."

"Well done," answered Stan. Then he stopped, with a sudden feeling of sadness. This would be the most final of all goodbyes. He would never see Targ again. Come to think of it, he had never seen him at all. But they had shared many adventures, and he had come to think of Targ as a real friend.

"We shall not meet again," said Targ, his high-pitched voice sounding chilly and remote. "The planet Earth is too primitive a society to be of interest to the Galactic Community. Perhaps, when Earth dwellers have solved the problems of war, disease, poverty and environmental pollution, another Pathfinder may come this way. But it is time for us to say goodbye."

Stan glowered disappointedly at the screen. Targ seemed to have no feelings at all. He had been scared enough during their search for the Gem of Power. Why couldn't he be just a little grateful now?

"I owe you my life," Targ went on, as if reading Stan's thoughts, "and for that I give you my heartfelt thanks. From now on, although we live at opposite ends of the galaxy, we shall always be friends. Try to think of me when you look up into the sky, and I shall do the same on Karothan. Now I have one last duty to request of you. Wait for the sudden flicker of your house lights that will signal my departure, then switch off your computer."

"I'm ready," Stan told him, a bit shaken by the realization that he was going to miss Targ very much. "Safe journey. Goodbye."

"Goodbye, Stan," said Targ.

Stan sat quite still, watching the screen intently. Targ's ★ symbol shimmered and seemed to merge into the space craft. There was a moment's pause, then the house lights flickered sharply and the screen went blank. Targ had launched himself into space. Feeling suddenly lonely, Stan switched off the computer and went downstairs.

At school, a few weeks later, the Head stood up in a crowded assembly hall to make an important announcement.

"I can now tell you the name of the winner of the holiday competition," he said. "But before I do so, I wish to thank the school governors who acted as independent judges."

A chorus of boos came from the middle of the hall, and a squadron of paper aeroplanes made crash landings on the front row. The staff, lined up on a row of chairs behind the Head, made disapproving faces. The boos got louder.

"The entries were so good that the judges had a difficult time," the Head went on, raising his voice against the hubbub, "but in the end one entry stood out above all the others."

"Well, go on then, tell us," blared out a

voice.

"Cor, this is taking forever," complained another.

"It was perhaps rather crudely written," the Head plugged on doggedly, trying to ignore the interruptions, "but what impressed the judges was that it was clearly the person's own work, done without any outside help. So without further ado, I am pleased to announce that the winner of the holiday competition is . . . " He made a sudden signal to Miss Perkins, who was seated at the piano on one side of the platform. Miss Perkins banged out a thunderous chord. ". . . Stanley Wheeler!" declared the Head.

Stan nearly fell off his chair. Somebody pushed him to his feet. He trudged up to the platform in a dream. The Head shook him warmly by the hand and gave him the envelope containing the free holiday tickets for the next school trip abroad. On the way back to his seat, Stan saw Mr Bartlett staring at him with a funny look on his face. Mr Bartlett could see promotion coming his way. His expression was that of a starving vulture who has just spotted a good feed. But Stan wasn't to know that.

At breaktime, the Raiders clustered round Stan to collect their share of the prize.

"No need to be scared, Stan," growled Billy Regan, waggling fingers as big as bananas under Stan's nose. "Just hand over the free tickets."

"Yeh, before we turn you into a nasty mess on the playground," grunted Flatnose Biggs.

"Or think up something even worse to do to you," giggled Blinker Price.

Stan felt his knees go wobbly, but he made himself look calmy back at them. "Remember when you came up to my house and took my computer disks?" he asked.

"'Course we do. What about it?" snarled Regan.

"There was a removal van in the street," said Stan. "A new family was getting ready to move in. Since then they've arrived."

"What's that got to do with anything?" demanded Regan.

"Look behind you," replied Stan.

The Raiders turned round. Behind them

were standing three hefty teenagers. They had broad shoulders, square chins and a steely glint in their eyes.

"Meet my new friends and neighbours, the Clark brothers," said Stan cheerfully. "I'm going to share the tickets with them." The Clark brothers stepped forward. The Raiders hastily stepped back.

"Just push off!" Stan told the Raiders. "And if you've got any sense, you'll leave me alone."

He watched the Raiders slink away across the playground. Then he gave the Clark brothers a grin. Life was going to be a lot better from now on.

JUGGLERS

There are books to suit everyone in Hippo's JUGGLERS series:

When I Lived Down Cuckoo Lane
by Jean Wills   £1.75
A small girl and her family move into a new house in Cuckoo Lane. Follow her adventures through the year as she makes friends, starts a new school, learns to ride a bike, and even helps out at her father's shop.

The Secret of Bone Island by Sam McBratney   £1.75
Linda, Peter and Gareth are very curious about Bone Island. Especially when they're told some weird stories about the island's history. And then three suspicious-looking men warn them to stay away from the island . . .

Stan's Galactic Bug by John Emlyn Edwards   £1.75
Stan can't believe his eyes when his computer game traps an alien from outer space. It's up to Stan to save the intergalactic traveller from destruction!

As If By Magic by Jo Furminger   £1.75
Natasha has never seen a girl as weird as Harriet – the new girl in the class. But not only does she *look* strange, with her dark tatty clothes and bright green eyes, but the oddest things start to happen when she's around.

Look out for these other titles in the JUGGLERS series:

Bags of Trouble by Michael Harrison
The Jiggery-Pokery Cup by Angela Bull

STREAMERS

We've got lots of great books for younger readers in Hippo's STREAMERS series:

Sally Ann – On Her Own by Terrance Dicks   £1.75
Sally Ann is a very special toy. She's a rag doll who likes to be involved in everything that's going on. When Sally Ann finds out that the nursery school where she lives might be closed down, she decides it's time to take action!

Sally Ann – The School Play by Terrance Dicks £1.75
When the nursery school's electricity goes off, Sally Ann comes up with a wonderful idea to pay for the new wiring. But not everything runs as smoothly as Sally Ann would like!

The Little Yellow Taxi and His Friends
by Ruth Ainsworth   £1.75
The little grey car can't get to sleep at night, and keeps all the other cars and lorries awake. So the garage owner paints the little car yellow, gives him a sign for his roof, and turns him into an all-night taxi.

Tom by Ruth Silvestre   £1.75
The circus has come to town, and Tom tries to tell his parents about it. But they are always too busy to listen. . .
A delightful collection of stories about Tom, his family and friends.

Look out for these other titles in the STREAMERS series:

Nate the Great by Marjorie Sharmat
Nate the Great and the Missing Key by Marjorie Sharmat

MARLENE MARLOWE INVESTIGATES

My name is Marlene. Marlene Marlowe. And I'm the dottiest detective ever to have missed a clue . . .

Follow the hilarious trail of the world's most clueless private eye in these books by Hippo:

Marlene Marlowe Investigates the Great Christmas Pudding Mystery £1.75
Early one morning Marlene is woken by a phonecall: "Come to Peregrine Postlethwaite's bakery immediately!" In the dimly-lit building Marlene follows a trail of dark red sticky mess, leading to a large moving bundle . . .

Marlene Marlowe Investigates the Missing Tapes Affair £1.75
A phonecall summons Marlene to the house of an old friend. There, slumped on the kitchen floor, lies the twisted body of a young man . . .

You'll find these and many more great Hippo books at your local bookseller, or you can order them direct. Just send off to *Customer Services, Hippo Books, Westfield Road, Southam, Leamington Spa, Warwickshire CV33 OJH*, not forgetting to enclose a cheque or postal order for the price of the book(s) plus 30p per book for postage and packing.

HIPPO BOOKS FOR OLDER READERS

If you enjoy a really good read, look out for all the Hippo books that are available right now. You'll find gripping adventure stories, romance novels, spooky ghost stories and all sorts of fun fiction to keep you glued to your book!

HAUNTINGS: Ghost Abbey by Robert Westall £1.95
The Little Vampire in Love
by Angela Sommer-Bodenberg   £1.25
Snookered by Michael Hardcastle   £1.50
Palace Hill by Peter Corey   £1.95
Black Belt by Nicholas Walker   £1.75
STEPSISTERS 1: The War Between the
Sisters by Tina Oaks   £1.75
THE MALL 1: Setting Up Shop
by Carolyn Sloan   £1.75
Conrad's War by Andrew Davies   £1.75
Cassie Bowen Takes Witch Lessons by Anna
Grossnickle Hines   £1.75
Tales for the Midnight Hour by J B Stamper £1.75
Creeps by Tim Schock   £1.50

You'll find these and many more fun Hippo books at your local bookshop, or you can order them direct. Just send off to *Customer Services, Hippo Books, Westfield Road, Southam, Leamington Spa, Warwickshire CV33 0JH*, not forgetting to enclose a cheque or postal order for the price of the book(s) plus 30p per book for postage and packing.

HIPPO BOOKS FOR YOUNGER READERS

If you've enjoyed this book, you'll probably be interested to know that there are loads more Hippo books to suit all kinds of tastes. You'll find scary spooky books, gripping adventure stories, funny books, and lots lots more.

You'll find these and many more fun Hippo books at your local bookshop, or you can order them direct. Just send off to *Customer Services, Hippo Books, Westfield Road, Southam, Leamington Spa, Warwickshire CV33 OJH*, not forgetting to enclose a cheque or postal order for the price of the book(s) plus 30p per book for postage and packing.